Charles Larcom Graves

The Green above the Red

More Blarney Ballads

Charles Larcom Graves

The Green above the Red
More Blarney Ballads

ISBN/EAN: 9783743300057

Manufactured in Europe, USA, Canada, Australia, Japa

Cover: Foto ©Andreas Hilbeck / pixelio.de

Manufactured and distributed by brebook publishing software
(www.brebook.com)

Charles Larcom Graves

The Green above the Red

THE

GREEN ABOVE THE RED

More Blarney Ballads

BY

CHARLES L. GRAVES

AUTHOR OF "THE BLARNEY BALLADS"

WITH ILLUSTRATIONS BY LINLEY SAMBOURNE

London

SWAN SONNENSCHEIN & CO.

PATERNOSTER SQUARE

1889

PREFACE.

SOME of the following verses have already seen the light in various London and provincial papers, and I have to express my indebtedness to the editors of the *Spectator, Globe, Manchester Examiner, Yorkshire Post, Irish Times, Union,* and *Liberal Unionist,* for their kind permission to reprint them. I have stated the nature of my obligation to Mr. Wilfrid Blunt's prison poems on p. 47, but it is right to add to that general statement the confession that the title and metre of " Remember O'Brien " are borrowed from one of his pieces.

C. L. G.

CONTENTS.

vii

ILLUSTRATIONS.

THE

GREEN ABOVE THE RED.

⚓be fIDarcb of tbe fIDan of Ibawarben.

Man of Hawarden! march to glory,
O'er the corpse of Whig and Tory;
Recreant Balfour, gaunt and gory,
    Shudders at the shock.
Raise, O labyrinthine talker,
Raise your battle cry of " Walker!"
Emulate the licensed hawker,
    Or the Gallic cock.
    Come, a truce to lagging,
    Set your tongue a-wagging,
Till the foe dissolves like snow
    Before your bally-ragging.
March along through wreck and rapine,
With your emerald banner flappin';
Flesh your brand-new axe by Mappin;
    Stop the Union Clock!

Man of Hawarden ! upward popping,
Tell again the tale of Dopping,
Spread it wide from Wick to Wapping,
    In the richest brogue.
Stir your stumps a little smarter,
Scratch the Russ and show the Tartar,
Hook some fresh-run English martyr—
    " Kelts " are out of vogue.
        See, the tide is flowing,
        And the leek is blowing ;
Let the wail of Innisfail
        Set Cambria's pulses glowing.
Prove, by clearest demonstration,
Taffy's trifling depredation
Was the shameless fabrication
    Of some Saxon rogue.

Man of Hawarden ! see, Saint George is
Powerless to control the orgies
Of the Dragon, who disgorges
    Floods of greenest gall.
What are " thousands " against " millions," *
Hartingtons against Trevelyans,
Madrigals to Welsh Penillions,

---

* Mr. Caine said there were three hundred thousand Liberal Unionists ;
but he (Mr. H. Gladstone) thought a liberal allowance would be one-half of
that, whilst their own ranks were numbered by millions, and how could the
millions be said to desert the thousands ?—Speech of Mr. Herbert Gladstone
at Chester. *Standard,* October 30, 1888.

Barnabas to Paul ?
Rend the realm asunder,
Glut the poor with plunder,
Hurl the rich into the ditch
And " keep " their " proud souls under " :
Cast aside all moderation,
And achieve, with exultation,
England's utter uncreation—
England's final fall !

"You are old, Father William."

"You are old, Father William," began the boy,
    "Yet I'm sure, on consid'ring the question,
You can swallow things whole that would simply destroy
    Ev'n a boa-constrictor's digestion."

"In the days of my youth," sighed the sage from his book—
    "Let the cause your attention engage—
I gave thirty-three chews to each mouthful I took,
    To prepare for the pleasures of age."

"You are old, Father William," resumed the youth,
    "And yet I observe with surprise,
That, although you can never stop opening your mouth,
    You keep constantly closing your eyes."

"The answer is simpler than you'd have supposed :—
    When a quite inexperienced man,
With my weather-eye open, my weather-mouth closed,
    I pursued just the opposite plan.

"But a prophet whose aquiline vision absorbs
    The future through ages unsung
May be freely forgiven for veiling his orbs
    And setting the spurs to his tongue."

" You are old, Father William," persisted the boy,
     " Yet you *do* so delight in a ' dopper,'
That, till threatened by law, you refuse to withdraw :—
     At your age is that decent or proper ? "

Quoth the sage, " In my youth, to the dictates of truth
     I adhered with such hearty conviction,
That I surely may pay, now I'm aged and grey,
     An occasional tribute to fiction."

" You are old, Father William——" " Dry up," said the sage,
     " And be off out of that in a jiffy ;
Cut your Brummagem stick, or I'll catch you a kick
     That'll hoist you from here to the Liffey."

𝔚illiam's 𝔚ain;

OR,

THE LOSS OF THE VAN-GUARD.

Vanitas vanitatum.—*Ecclesiastes.*
Mystica vannus Iacchi.—*Virg.*

[Until the autumn of 1888 Mr. Patrick Murray was engaged in driving a
Home Rule Union Van about the country, and was described in placards
and advertisements as having "left the Royal Irish Constabulary rather than
take part in evictions." A question put in the House of Commons elicited
the information that, while nobody answering to that name had *resigned*,
three men, all called Patrick Murray, had been *discharged* from the force in
the last three years. Further inquiries identified the Home Rule Van-driver
with the individual who was discharged from the force with a gratuity, in
August, 1887, as unfit for further service owing to an affection of the brain.
In spite of this, however, his employers have dispensed with his services.]

I who drive this Parnellite four-wheeler,
    Jarvey of this green Gladstonian fly,
I was once a base, a blood-stained peeler,
    Of the deepest, darkest, deadliest dye ;
Once I was a mercenary minion,
    Revelling in the sight of needless pain ;
Now there breathes not any Abyssinian
    More undeviatingly humane.
Yes, I am a peaceful missionáry
    " Moving on " from Beersheba to Dan,
And no matter how our fortunes vary,
    I at least am always in the Van.

Should you ask what cleansed my soul Satanic,
  What induced this startling change of front,—
'Twas a wave of influence galvanic
  Flowing from the frame of Wilfrid Blunt ;
For at Woodford, as he held his mission,
  I was one of that benighted horde
Who—I own it with profound contrition—
  Hustled the apostle overboard.
But the martyr, mangled and disjointed,
  Showed, as only Orientals can,
Marvellous forbearance, and appointed
  Me as driver of the Home Rule Van.

Once I twirled the terrifying truncheon,
  Once I plied the barbarous battering-ram ;
Now I'm asked to Dollis Hill to luncheon
  And discuss the genesis of jam.
Once I was a loyal salamander,
  Facing showers of scalding stirabout ;
Now I wage undying war on slander,
  And demolish " Philosophic Doubt."
Once our patriots' lips I placed the gag on,
  Once I did my best to wreck the Plan ;
Now I navigate the Home Rule wagon,
  Now I ride triumphant in the Van.

Balfour, like a truculent garroter,
  In the *Times* my sanity derides ;
Oh, he'll find the situation hotter
  When I've raised my corps of *Murray's Guides!*

Then along the Severn and the Humber,
　　Then along the Isis and the Trent,
We will neither slacken rein nor slumber,
　　Ventilating Erin's discontent.
Yes, wherever local irritation
　　Rears itself against the tyrant's ban,
Counselling conspicuous moderation,
　　Each of us will skirmish in his Van.
　　　　　*　　　*　　　*　　　*　　　*

What! you think "on due consideration"
　　That you won't "require me any more"?
Tare an' ouns! this bangs the whole creation;
　　Sure I never heard the likes before!
O ye blathering Separatist varmints,
　　May disaster dog your crazy track;
Give me my constabulary garments,
　　Give me belt and give me carbine back!
May the devil drive your dirty party
　　Horse and foot to China or Japan!
What's the use of Parnell and M'Carthy,
　　When there's no one left to guide the Van?

ₐ ffancy Portrait.

Let me sing to you of Cony—
    Courteous Conybeare ;
He's no fashionable " Johnny,"
    Never, never fear ;
Nor a Piccadilly dandy ;
But he's loved by dear old Sandy
    With a love sincere ;
And he's dear to gallant Taffy—
Were I gifted as Mahaffy,
    I could tell how dear ;
Gentle Cony—genial Cony—
    Gracious Conybeare !

He was trained at Oxford, Cony—
    Clever Conybeare,
Where he utterly astoni—
    Stonishèd his year ;
Not by loud nocturnal screeches,
Nor by variegated breeches,
But by trenchant Union speeches,
    Drawing many a tear
From the eyes of dons and doctors,
Deans, pro-consuls, and pro-proctors.
    Oh, a bright career

All predicted for their Cony—
    Clever Conybeare!

Long and loyally he studied
    With a zeal severe,
Till his genius bloomed and budded,—
    Patient Conybeare!
He was not an office-seeker,
But he yearned to beard the Speaker,
    Yearned to hurl his spear
'Mid the Unionist debaters,
Yearned to rout the Tory praters,
    Crush the fopling peer:
Balmy, bouncing, Tory-trouncing,
    Flouncing Conybeare!

Then the Scions of Trelawny,
    Void of all veneer,
Cornish giants, grim and brawny,
    Called for Conybeare;
And he left the home of syntax
For the land of tin and tin-tacks,
    Quite a different sphere;
And the miners, in their millions,
From their underground pavilions,
Some on foot and more on pillions,
Come to meet him, with postillions
    And the grenadier—
No, a *German* band for Cony -
    Happy Conybeare!

Had I but the brush of Sambourne,
    Or of Edward Lear,
I would limn the pride of Camborne,
    Lovely Conybeare ;
Vieing, in his grace of manner,
With angelic Doctor Tanner,
    Noble cavalier !
Parrying Balfour's poisoned rapier
With the *sang-froid* of a Napier,
    Or a Vere de Vere :
Seldom vicious, dear, delicious,
    Bonny Conybeare !

Three Political Villanelles.

I.—VILLANELLE OF THE OLD MAN OF THE SEA.

I'm the Grandest Old Man of the Sea
    That Bull ever took on his back.
My bonnet's the home of the bee.

I'm quite at the top of the tree :
    For my age I'm remarkably sprack.
I'm the Grandest Old Man of the Sea.

I dwell on the banks of the Dee :
    I'm partial to ' O' ' and to ' Mac.'
My bonnet's the home of the bee.

Poor Paddy's devoted to me,
    I'm glad he gave Sackville the sack.
I'm the Grandest Old Man of the Sea.

I'm fond of my five o'clock tea :
    I'm fonder of Green than of Black.
My bonnet's the home of the bee.

If I live to a hundred and three,
    I shall haul down the Union Jack.
I'm the Grandest Old Man of the Sea.
My bonnet's the home of the bee.

II.—VILLANELLE OF THE OLD PARLIA-
MENTARY HAND.

I'M an Old Parliamentary Hand ;
    I've swallowed the Plan of Campaign,
But I don't like the lie of the land.

I feel both for Tanner and Tanned ;
    I know that the Celt is humane.
I'm an Old Parliamentary Hand.

I've plotted and striven and planned
    To unravel this tangled skein ;
But I don't like the lie of the land.

Bereft of old friends I stand :
    The Tories compare me to Cain.
I'm an Old Parliamentary Hand.

Am I building upon the sand ?
    I can count on O'Brien and Blaine,
But I don't like the lie of the land.

I am Old ; am I *really* Grand ?
    Is my castle in Wales or Spain ?
I'm an Old Parliamentary Hand,
But I don't like the lie of the land.

III.—VILLANELLE OF THE LOYAL JACKASS

I'M sick of Harcourt's sounding brass,
  Of Morley's tinkling symbolism.
Why am I such a loyal ass ?

I wish they'd put me out to grass
  Far from this everlasting schism.
I'm sick of Harcourt's sounding brass.

My features in the looking-glass
  Seem sicklied o'er with pessimism.
Why am I such a loyal ass ?

I flounder in the rank morass
  Of Separatist syllogism.
I'm sick of Harcourt's sounding brass.

The Parnellites are not first-class :
  Their creed's the rankest Communism.
Why am I such a loyal ass ?

I cannot worship with the mass :
  I can't endure this fetishism.
I'm sick of Harcourt's sounding brass.
Why am I such a loyal ass ?
              Echo : Ass !

Rides to Power.

A Rondeau.

[" He even alluded to ' three acres and a cow,' regarding which he should
have been silent, for he rose to power upon that unfortunate animal, and
then turned her out to starve—nothing more being heard of the cow while
his Administration continued."—*Mr. Goschen at West Bromwich, Nov.* 14,
1888.]

To ride to power, ten years ago,
On my Bulgarian buffalo,
   At Dizzy and the Golden Horn
   I tilted, one election morn,
And routed Turk and Tory foe.
Experiencing an overthrow,
I changed my mount, and *then*, you know,
   On Collings' cow I thought no scorn
     To ride to power.
But as I crossed St. Stephen's flow,
I swapped her, spite of Lincoln's *mot*,
   For Erin's Bull, and WE are sworn,
   Upon that green-eyed monster borne,
WE—GLADSTONE, PARNELL, FORD, and Co.,—
     To ride to power.

Lines by a "Blind Admirer."

[It was stated in a well-known Russophil evening paper—the *Pellmellikoff Gazetzky*—on the occasion of Mr. Gladstone's visit to Birmingham in November, 1888, that applications for tickets had been received not only from the *blind*, but the *deaf and the dumb*. And a *bonâ fide* letter from a "Blind Admirer" of Mr. Gladstone's was quoted in their columns.]

GREAT leader, whose aquiline optic *
    Fate wills that I ne'er may behold,
Quit the study of Erse and of Coptic,
    Leave Olympus awhile in the cold :
Let thy voice, like the call of a clarion,
    Bring balm to the deaf and the dumb ;
Swoop down on the Unionist carrion,
    And scatter the scum.

We are sick of the sermons of Otto,
    Of Harcourt's elaborate † jeers ;
Thou only, rhetorical Giotto,
    Canst argue in absolute spheres.

---

* *Aquiline optic:* Eagle eye (Lat. *aquila*). Others wrongly derive from *Aquilo*, the blusterous wind, and quote the well-known phrase "Gladstonian windbag." The following quotation is, however, conclusive against this :— "I want to have his eagle eye meet mine."—*Pellmellikoff Gazetzky.*

† *Elaborate:* Vide "labor improbus" (*Virg.*).

Too long with Elizabeth's era,
   With religious romance hast thou toyed ;
Come forth, O consummate Chimæra,*
   And boom in the void !

Our love of the truth, pray remember,
   Is earnest, but O is it right
To drag her, in chilly November,
   Unclothed to the merciless light ?
So be true to thy training ; be subtle :
   Let no one thy meaning divine :
Yea, put forth the craft of the cuttle,
      And blacken the brine.

We are weary and faint with pursuing
   Humanity's uniform track ;
Great Anarch ! be up and undoing,
   Set the dial a century back.
Hark ! in tune to the tocsin of treason
   Our infants in unison lisp,
" Come down and redeem us from reason,
      Great Will o' the Wisp ! "

---

* *Consummate Chimæra :* Cf. the parody upon scholastic disputations by Erasmus. *Quæritur " an Chimæra, bombinans in vacuo, possit devorare secundas intentiones."*

Lines to Lord Macaulay's Biographer.

[Sir George Trevelyan, in a letter recently addressed to a correspondent, who had written to him for some information about Macaulay, spoke of the 'rush of regret" that had come over him in being thus suddenly recalled from politics to literature.]

O INCOMPREHENSIBLE Otto,
    Once famed for your whimsical grace,
Can it be that your family motto *
    Is proving its truth in your case?
Are the terms of surrender too galling,
    Are the fetters beginning to fret,
That you plaintively speak of your falling
    A prey to regret?

Yes, a "rush of regret" has assailed you,
    A dissatisfaction divine;
Infatuate Otto! what ailed you
    Your earlier *rôle* to resign?
What ailed you, infatuate Otto,
    To stray from your studious retreat?—
Like a sensitive plant from a grotto,
    Cast into the street.

* Time trieth troth.

Oh, why, in biography peerless,
   Did you barter your lettered repose
For a life that is chequered and cheerless—
   A life of unlimited prose ?
For it can't have been craving for shekels,
   And it can't have been family pride,
That drove you, the gentlest of Jekylls,
     To emulate Hyde!

What caused you, O trimmest of trimmers,
   To swerve and to sway in your gait ?—
Was it reading political primers
   That addled your eminent pate ?
Oh, to think of your finding a haven
   Beneath the Gargantuan gamp !—
Like Samson, insidiously shaven
     In the Philistine camp.

With your Fox you made excellent running,
   Now a goose-chase is wasting your breath :
Oh, pursue with your earlier cunning,
   And you're sure to be in at the death !
Leave the limbo of dumps and of dudgeon,
   Quit the mighty Milesian stew,
Cast aside your political bludgeon,
     Wield the rapier anew.

Like a prodigal, sick of the diet
  Of Paddy's perpetual stye,
Too husky to rant or to riot,
  For liberal leisure you sigh.
Oh, come back to the calm of the cloister,
  Give your erudite energies scope ;
Leave the workaday world—'tis an oyster
  You never will ope.

Ibome Rule Aroon!

OR,

THE LAY OF THE DISLOYAL JACKASS.

(To the Air of "Shule Aroon.")

I WOULD I were in yonder House!
'Tis there I sit, mute as a mouse,
Until the season of the grouse.
　　Chorus.—Home Rule, Rule, Aroon!

I guessed the way the cat would jump;
I parted from the Tory "Rump,"
And went round Ireland on the stump.
　　Chorus.—Home Rule, Rule, Aroon!

I turned my coat from blue to green;
I spoke unkindly of the Queen;
I witnessed an eviction scene.
　　Chorus.—Home Rule, Rule, Aroon!

I stood again, but, cursèd luck!
Our glorious leader ran amuck,
And in the Irish gutter stuck.
　　Chorus.—Home Rule, Rule, Aroon!

I wish, I wish, I wish in vain,
I wish I had my seat again ;
I think I must have been insane.
      Chorus.—Home Rule, Rule, Aroon !

Oh, Fire and Fury seize the " Plan " :
Confusion take that Green Old Man :—
Why did I leave the frying-pan ?
      Chorus.—Home Rule, Rule, Aroon !

The Magic Lantern.

[*Scene.*—A lecture hall in the Black Country, profusely decorated with bunting and Dis-Union Jacks emblazoned with crownless harps, Manx cats, and Welsh rabbits. In the reserved seats are to be noticed Sir U. Cole-Scuttleworth, and other local magnates. The body of the hall is crowded with a packed and enthusiastic audience. On the platform at the back a large white sheet, in front to the right a table, to the left an upright Collard pianoforte. Enter the Lecturer. Prolonged enthusiasm. Cheers, tears, and laughter. Also Hymns, Ancient and Modern,—especially modern. Presentation, by members of the Gladstone-Tanner Branch of the Gaelic Athletic Association, of a pair of bog-oak dumb-bells, and a pat of Irish butter. Serenade by the ham-strung band of the Fir-Bolgic Invincibles.]

LADIES and Gentlemen, your cheers,
Ringing on my grateful ears,
Prove that though I've lost the trust
Of the hardened Upper Crust,
I have struck the softest parts
Of the people's pudding hearts.

Ne'er can I the exchange regret,
Ne'er discharge the heavy debt
That hermetically seals
William to your chariot wheels.
Yet, perchance, he may be able,
Ere he leaves this lecture table,
With his lantern just a little
From that heavy debt to whittle.

Now observe this instrument :
Half a life-time I have spent,
In the workshop and the mine,
Puzzling out its deep design ;
Till at last the conscious spark
Clove the circumambient dark,
Signalling my sanguine soul
To its great and glorious goal.
Let me now to every eye
How it acts exemplify.
Ilka lad and lassie kens
That an ordinary lens
Can the vulgar fancy cheat
By reflections on a sheet ;
But I claim for *my* machine,
As I'll show upon that screen,
That no lantern ever lit
Can at all compare with it :
For, as presently I'll show,
It will make an object grow,
Till its just and true proportions
End in most grotesque contortions.
Thus, a mole-hill on my slide
To a mountain's magnified,
Towering and towering still
Over an undoubted hill.
If, upon the other hand,
Diminution you demand,
At a glance Mount Everest

To a mole-hill is compressed.
Then again to garish glints
It can quicken neutral tints,
Or the flush of summer sober
To the flickerings of October.
Nay, from nothing this machine
Can create what should have been,
And present it with such force,
It becomes a thing of course.

I have various other views,
But to-night my Irish stews,—
Since I gather that you wish
For that favourite standing dish,—
On the canvas I propose
In due order to disclose.

First of all my specimens,
Lo! I throw upon the lens
One of Michael Davitt's " pens,"
On a piece of cartridge paper :
Well! I light it with this taper,
When, by means of this extension
Exercise you heard me mention—
See, hey presto! here's Mat Harris
And his sporting friends from Paris,
With their Irish country cousins,
Shooting landlords down by dozens !

That is Matthew—*those* his cartridges ;
This his bag of human " partridges."

After that abrupt *crescendo*,
Here's a choice *diminuendo !*
For I throw upon the screen
This Jack-ass steeped in paraffin,
Then by miscreants set a-flame,
As the credulous Tories claim.
Sprinkle some " Insanitas "
On that agonizing ass,
And the fiendish conflagration
Underneath the preparation
Soon begins to peak and pine
In a galloping decline,
Till quite " venially," my friends,
Look ! it " deviates " and ends
In the donkey, one Mick Davin
Fired for ring-bone or for spavin.

Now two contrasts let me choose
Out of my dissolving views.
Here's a cottage, at first sight
Seeming cosy, clean, and bright,
Standing in a homestead fine,
Cropped by pasturing sheep and kine.
Mark its inmates—see, they sit ;
Is there any doubt of it ?—
Chubby children, parents hearty,

Quite a model household party,
At their meal of beans and bacon ;—
You are *utterly mistaken.*
Look, my friends, a little nearer,
While I make that picture clearer.
Can it brook the influence bright
Of my magnifying light ?
Take the cottage : after all,
What we thought its stone-set wall,
Tidy tiles and glittering glass,
Into gaunt mud-misery pass.
Here's no chimney but the door,
Here's no table but the floor,
Where poor starving wretches squat
Round the seed-potato pot.
Crop and pasture, flock and herd,
Melt in mockery absurd
To one patch of sorry oats,
And two nibbling nanny-goats.

The difference I could always see
'Twixt Tweedledum and Tweedledee ;
But to-night I'll show you some
'Twixt Tweedledum and Tweedledum.

Here's Tweedledum, with smiling malice,
Passing round the poisoned chalice
That consigns with purpose fell
All the Sassenach spawn to Hell.

Hear him, now that game is up,
Sobbing o'er the loving cup,
"Saxon, we too long have striven,
Let's forgive and be forgiven."

Here's Tiny Tim, in wig and gown,
With a case against the Crown,
Arguing Roche's jurisdiction
Cannot set the least restriction
On such epithets as "sneak,"
Hurled against a hireling Beak.
Study Tim's forensic phiz,
And you'll find his dander's riz.
By two lengthy limbs of law,—
Since that sneak he won't withdraw,—
Timothy is now withdrawn,
Like an apprehensive prawn
Parrying with frantic feelers
All the onslaughts of its peelers!

Last, the O'Brien Blatherum,
Biting his tremendous thumb
At the lily-livered Thugs
Guarding Judas's stone-jugs:
Now engaged, at desperate odds,
For his breeches and his gods,
Wildly waging, one to four,
Furious battle on the floor;
Till at last, o'erpowered and peeled,

Panting, he his pants must yield ;
Yet this prophecy puffs and blows
In the faces of his foes :
" Fiends, I solemnly assert,
Sitting shivering in my shirt,
Since tit for tat our history teaches,
Be it so ! for breeches, breaches ;
From our Yankee Irrepressibles
Pitiless retaliations ;
For my shattered ' inexpressibles '
Clerkenwell continuations ;
Till the Union Jack goes down
Before the Harp without the Crown,
And Erin through the welkin wags
Emblazoned with O'Brien's bags ! "

CURTAIN.

The Sassenach Samson.

(*To the Air of " The Protestant Gun."*)

[Suggested by Sir Henry James's comparison of a well-known Liberal politician to Samson with a wig on.]

THERE are threasures in Ulster as good as our own,
For we're sucking the Orange as dry as a bone,
And this Sassenach Samson,—more power to his jaw!—
Shouts "Hurroo for ould Ireland!" and "Down wid the
    law!"
Yet four short years ago, ere we cropped his love-locks,
Man alive! sure he dealt us the divil's hard knocks:
But we've hauled down his colours and altered his rig,
And giv'n poor ould Samson a wonderful wig.

'Tis grand to see Blunt standing up for the " Plan,"
Wid himself in the rear and his wife in the van:
There's pleasure in capping a colleen wid pitch,
Or in stripping a bailiff of ivery stitch:
'Tis sweet to give grabbers a taste of cold lead,
To boycott them living and boycott them dead:
But for all these divarsions I'd not give a fig,
After seeing ould Samson dressed out in a wig.

I've laughed till I felt I was ready to split
At Gladstone bla'guárding the measures of Pitt;

Or at Sullivan swearing he's fit for to burst
Wid the love of a nation he formerly cursed ;
Or at Dillon the dauntless, who lately was seen
Dancing Kitchin quadrilles wid a Protestant Dean :
But of all these performances, little or big,
None aiquals ould Samson dressed out in his wig.

The Union of Hearts.

WHAT boots it, dissentient battalions,
　　Of your birth and your breeding to brag,—
To label us ragged rapscallions,
　　Needy knights of the green carpet bag ?
Though fools by fine feathers be flattered,
　　Snobs snared by Society's arts,
The Union of Caste shall be shattered
　　By the Union of Hearts.

Girt around by your Stars and your Garters,
　　Pert plank-bedding props of the Pale,
Ye rudely ride over our charters,
　　Ye lock up our leaders in gaol.
Mad Marquis, your vessel, dismasted,
　　Drifts to doom without compass or charts,
For the Union of Rank shall be blasted
　　By the Union of Hearts.

Ye have millionaires rolling in riches,
　　Ye count on the clan of the Guelph,
Whilst our champions are robbed of their breeches
　　And poorly provided with pelf :
Yet muster the minions of Mammon,
　　Make the most of the monarchs of marts,
For the Union of Gold is as gammon
　　To the Union of Hearts.

Ye are sharper than Thackeray's Becky,
    We do not disparage your wit;
We envy you Dicey and Lecky,
    And Joseph resigned to his Pitt :
Your learning is deep and undoubted,
    Ye are men of remarkable parts,
But the Union of Heads shall be routed
    By the Union of Hearts.

Then avaunt, ye Coercionist croakers,
    For staunch and unshaken remains
The Alliance of Porridge and Pokers,
    Against the assemblage of Brains :
Our flag no surrender shall sully,
    No shield stay our death-dealing darts,
For our war-cries are " Tanner and Tully !
    And " The Union of Hearts ! "

The Chaunt of the Bronze Mask.

[Shortly before Mr. Gladstone's departure for Italy in December, 1888, the parishioners of a well-known London clergyman presented him with a bronze mask of Mr. Gladstone.]

Forgive, kind shade of Mackworth Praed,
One, who on wax-bound pinion
Essays a flight where you by right
Hold undisturbed dominion.

———

I THINK that at this festive time,
—This Saturnalian season,—
More folk will hearken to my rhyme
Than to my foeman's reason :
And so before I cross the wave
And quit this fog-wrapt city,
I'll sing you all a simple stave,—
A deviating ditty.

I think the style of Pitt and Peel
Intolerably uniform,
Ere rhetoricians learnt to deal
In cryptograms and cuneiform.
I think abruptness in a speech
An underbred atrocity,
And so I practise, as I preach,
Exuberant verbosity.

I think that Dillon's much maligned,
  That Blunt is most Quixotic ;—
Although his poetry I find
  A trifle too erotic.
I think the books of Mr. Bryce
  Are humorous and spicy ;
I think the use of loaded dice
  Appropriate to Dicey.

I think that Tanners should not stray
  Beyond their native tan-yards :
I think that Balfour, in his way,
  Exceeds the torturing Spaniards.
I think, whatever Parnell thinks
  Is due to Erin's pleading,
Although it snaps the latest links,
  There's reason for conceding.

I think that Ulster, loyal drudge,
  Could never wax rebellious :
I think by far the greatest judge
  Of jam is Aulus Gellius.
I think, ere Balfour drains the Bann,
  The Jews will drain the Jordan :
I think I'd tramp to the Soudan
  To lay the ghost of Gordon.

I think I have in Labouchere
  The aptest of my pupils,

Although he harbours, I'm aware,
    A plethora of scruples.
I think that Harcourt in his soul
    Must have a hidden inkling,
That, where full moonlight floods the pole,
    There's little need of " twinkling."

I think that I shall live to sing
    One day " In questa tomba "
Over the ruin of the Thing
    That I re-christened *Bomba.*
I think there's room for all, and scope
    Beneath my old umbrella :
I think that if I were the Pope,
    I'd canonize Kinsella.

I think the faithless R.I.C.
    A set of brutal bandits,
Who execute illegally
    Their lawless leader's mandates.
I think that quite the largest part
    Of those who wear the ermine
Are rotten to the very heart,
    And most unwholesome vermin.

I think, for his nutritious nibs,
    We all of us should bless Epps :
I think that for finance and fibs
    I flatten F. de Lesseps.

The music of the Shan Van Vocht
  I much prefer to Handel :
I think the game of Persico
  Not worth a Roman candle.

I think, compared to such a dad,
  Herbert's a hopeless oubit :
I think by thinking I can add
  My stature to a cubit.

  *   *   *   *   *

I think that as my cab is brought,
  And dallying's detrimental,
Unless I quit this train of thought,
  I'll miss the " Continental."

Thim's Tim's Sentiments.

O'CONNELL fenced too fairly for Repeal, boys;
　O'Connell's dead as mutton;
I much prefer to ply my savage steel, boys,
　Unguarded by a button.

O'Connell was a scurvy "single-drop" man;
　O'Connell's gone to glory;
But I'm a take-the-ball-upon-the-hop man,
　A hop however gory.

Vernon Avick!

(Dedicated without permission to the Author of "Father O'Flynn," by the Author of "The Blarney Ballads.")

Of all the gay " scions " and sprigs of nobility,
Far renowned for their grace and agility,
Faix I'd advance you for sheer volatility,
Vernon avick! as the flower of them all.
    Here's a health to you, Vernon avick!
    Long may you flounder through thin and through thick,
        Merriest mummer,
        And burliest " bummer," *
And loudest big drummer in Westminster Hall.

Don't talk of your sages and seers of antiquity,
Famous for rectitude—or for obliquity,
Faix an' the divils at mental ubiquity,
Vernon avick! would make hay of them all.
    Come, I'll wager that nobody quite
    Aiquals his elegant blatherumskite,
        Down from urbanity
        Into inanity,
Troth! and profanity—if he'd the call.

---

  * *Bummer.* Primarily an idle, worthless fellow. Now used in a political as well as a general sense, to denote the hireling or henchman of a party. *See* " Farmer's Americanisms."

Arrah, Vernon machree! what were Bottom or Puck to you?
Falstaff himself was a harmless ould buck to you;
Look how you gather the Radical ruck to you,
Wisha bad luck to you, Vernon avick!
    Still, for all you're the prince of buffoons,
    Gad! you've the dash of a troop of dragoons,
        Firing the flagging ones,
        Bolstering the bragging ones,
Leathering the lagging ones on wid the stick.

And though never crossing the confines of charity,
Still, in your moments of mammoth hilarity,
Who, without showing the direst disparity,
Vies in vulgarity, Vernon, with you?
    Once Sir Ughtred was minded to frown,
    Till this remark broke his prudery down—
        " Is it lave jollity
        All to the 'quality'?
Cannot we masses be mountebanks too?"
    Here's a health to you, Vernon avick!
    Long may you flounder through thin and through thick,
        Merriest mummer,
        And burliest " bummer,"
And loudest big drummer in Westminster Hall.

"VERNON AVICK!"

SELECTIONS FROM THE NEW *BILLIAD*.

1. Billy O'Brien.

(To the air of "Bryan O'Lynn.")

BILLY O'BRIEN had no breeches to wear,
But the Blarney girls wove him so splendid a pair,
Wan peep in the glass made his streamin' eyes shine,
"How they suit my complexion!" said Billy O'Brien.

Bill grew so wake on the Prison Board fare
That his friends vowed to view him would make a saint
  swear;
But the whole of the time he was starvin' to death
Bill was boltin' ham sandwiches under his breath.

Och! the people they sot up a wonderful shout
For a new Tug of War, whin their lad was let out;
For they knew that the Parlymint, Peelers, and Pope,
Must go down wid Bill grippin' their end of the rope.

Billy O'Brien kem into the Court,
Wid Tim Healy to show the Removables sport,
But when the big fools intherfared wid their noise,
He let himself out on leg-bail wid the boys.

Billy O'Brien disappeared in the dark
On Miss O'Neill's arm, like the dove from No'h's ark;
Till into Hulme Hall he shot up from the south,
Wid Erin's own olive-branch fast in his mouth.

And whin like a love-bird from Miss O'Neill's bakery
He flew to his feet, Jacob Bright, that kind Quaker, he
Blubbered and sobbed wid hysterical joy,
" Bil—ly O'Bri—en, Oh! Bil—ly, my boy ! "

'Twas then that dear turtle-dove fresh from Porthcawl
Unfolded his tale o'er the heads of them all,
And whin Manchester'd heard his sweet message of peace
She handed him over to Balfour's police.

Now Bill's back in jail in ondacent ondress,
And betune his torn breeks and the landlord's disthress,
 Twixt the Plan and the Man, 'pon my conscience I'm curst
If I rightly can tell you whose *rents* are the worst.

2. Remember O'Brien.

(A SONG FOR FEBRUARY, 1889.)

ERIN, wake! for maimed and maneless
  Lies your lion-hearted son ;
Simple, scholarly and stainless,
  Saint and soldier rolled in one.
  Howl and shriek and wail and whine
  For the shaving of O'Brine :
Gather in your market-places,
Heap hot coals upon your faces ;
  For the pride of Innisfail
  Paces shirtless in his jail.
Wake! Remember O'Brien !

He who at the hill of Dollis
  Loved *desipere in loco*,
Now must sip, his soul to solace,
  Vile and enervating cocoa.
  He who once on venison fed,
  Now must batten on brown bread,
And inadequately sate his
Appetite on boiled "pitaties,"
  Till his saintly stomach turns
  And for daintier diet yearns.
Wirrasthrue! for William O'Brien.

He who once in Tipperary
    Strove and struggled day and night
Till he lowered rents to prairie
    Value, lies in piteous plight :
    In a dungeon, deep and dank,
    He is pining on the plank.
He who bearded all the Cecils
Now with brawny warders wrestles,
    Till he falleth in a faint,
    And the sinners shear the saint.
Ochone ! for William O'Brien.

By the sunken Alabama,
By the Great Gun of Athlone,*
    By the love of melodrama
Bred in your Hibernian bone,
    Burst the bolts of the Bastille,
    Make the skinny Scotchman reel :
Pour your blood nor stint your riches
Till a thousand pairs of breeches
    (Spite of turnkeys fierce and fell)
    Fill the bare-legged patriot's cell.
Hurroo ! for William O'Brien.

* Cf. the historic curse, "May you be eternally crammed, jammed, and
rammed down the mouth of the Great Gun of Athlone." This historic piece
of ordnance has no connection with the "Canon of Aughrim," mentioned
in Mr. Blunt's *In Vinculis*.

Every man that has a penny
   Should invest in dynamite :
Up! ye kittens of Kilkenny,
   Fling yourselves into the fight :
   Whet your teeth and bare your nails,
   Tread upon each other's tails :
Raise a resolute, appalling,
Patriotic caterwauling,
   Till the Viceroy, sick at soul,
   Scuttles off to mind his coal.
Miaow! for William O'Brien.

Do not stick at scurvy trifles,
   Do not be content with speech ;
Point your pikes and load your rifles
   From the muzzle to the breech !
   Did not he, the stainless-souled,
   Languish in the collier's hold ?
Did not he, ere quitting Carrick,
Act more gallantly than Garrick ?
   Which of you can hold a candle
   To the latchet of his sandal ?
Pooh! Remember O'Brien !

Patriots, when the storm-clouds thicken
   Do not fear to bear the brunt :
Strike,—but mind you are not stricken ;
   Place your women in the front.
   Most heroic harlequins,
   Save your bacon, save your skins :

Capture bringeth not disaster
If ye stick, like sticking-plaster,
   To your shirts and nether hose.
   So shall Erin crush her foes,
Thanks to William O'Brien !

3. Dungeon Doggerel.

Being a Cycle of Sonnets composed in a spirit of disrespectful discipleship, after the perusal of Mr. Blunt's *In Vinculis.*

He Becometh Enamoured of Death.

NAKED I came into this witless world,
  And well-nigh naked for the nonce I tramp
  These bare, bleak boards, uncarpeted and damp,
But for the blanket round my shoulders furled.
The henchmen of Barabbas fiercely hurled
  Themselves upon me, till my senses fled ;
  And when life came again, my hapless head
Had lost the locks that round my temples curled.

O death, I much mislike thee ; yet, methinks,
  On certain terms I would not fear to meet thee ;
From thy fell pangs my stainless spirit shrinks,
  Yet if all men could see them, I would greet thee.
Yea, all I would renounce—love, life, and salary—
If, dying, I were sure of a good gallery.

But on Second Thoughts Decideth to Live.

Nay, I will live.   Why should I snuff life's candle,
  When, living, goodliest guerdon I may reap ?
  Why should I barter for death's leaden sleep
A life untarnished by the taint of scandal?
Why should I, like the Viking or the Vandal,
  Pour out my blood in a Quixotic quest,
  Unbraced, unbreeched, uncollared, and undrest,
A bootless eremite, *sans* shirt, *sans* sandal ?

Life be it then, for I am sweet and dear
  To nostrils in the which I lately stunk ;
Life, for I long to banquet with the peer
  I likened to the polecat and the skunk ;
Life, for I mean, though stripped and clipped and shorn,
To beard the Lion and the Unicorn.

He Rebuketh a Friend who Biddeth Him Take Comfort by the Sufferings of Others.

Talk not to me, entombed in this abyss,
  Of Christian martyrs, mangled by the beasts,
  Of living torches burnt at Nero's feasts,
Nor of the brazen bull of Phalaris.
Prate not, as though I were a schoolroom miss,
  Of Regulus, devoid of all apparel,
  Pierced by the knives within his rolling barrel,—
Compared to mine, a fate fulfilled with bliss.

What do I care for Roman, or Greek,
　　Or how they suffered and endured and died ?
Thus much I know : *my* tortures are unique ;
　　No saint was more completely crucified.*
O vile affront, like to a babe in bibs,
Compelled to drink these nauseating nibs.

He Successfully Resisteth an Attempt to Ascertain His Weight.

To-day a day of agony hath been :
　　For, catching me asleep—which was not fair—
　　Ten giant gaolers placed me in a chair,
And tried to weigh me, and there *was* a scene,
For I, albeit haggard, livid, lean,
　　Made such a gallant fight for the good cause,
　　That, bursting from my hellish captors' claws,
I utterly capsized the whole machine.

A hundred thousand Irishmen know well,—
　　Aye, to an ounce—the stones and pounds I scale ;
But they, true hearts, would sooner die than tell
　　To any foe of mine that wondrous tale.
Herein at least I triumph over fate ;
Balfour shall never know my fighting weight.

＊ *Vide* "Remember O'Brien " (*In Vinculis*, p. 19) :—
　　　"Ireland I plead before high heaven
　　　For your saint upon his cross."
It would appear that Mr. O'Brien has supplanted Arabi in the affections of Mr. Blunt. In *The Wind and the Whirlwind* there occurs a literary travesty of the crucifixion in which Arabi is the central figure.

E

He Receiveth a Packet of Surreptitious Sandwiches.

Fond pledges of a loving nation's trust,
 Sweet sandwiches, that some admirer threw
 So deftly that they fell adown the flue,
All packed in paper to defy the dust ;—
How good ye are ! how innocent of crust !
  And some are ham, and some again are tongue !
  Could Balfour see me, would he not be stung
With bitter disappointment and disgust !

But soft ! my sanguinary gaoler comes ;
 I hear a distant door's re-echoing slam ;
Quick ! let me gobble up yon tell-tale crumbs,
 Yon filmy fragment of delicious ham.
Come life, come death, whatever may betide,
At least my sandwiches are safe inside.

He Entertaineth a Visitor.

Condon, whom Fate imperiously hath called
 From cutting up the carcases of kine,
 To startle with thy eloquence divine
The Saxon senate, like an ancient Skald—
Livid and pale thou findest me, and mauled,
 For snicker-snack th' inexorable blade,
 As I lay fainting, round my temples played,
Till I revived, invincible but bald.

In Rome, 'tis said, when augurs met each other,
  They found it parlous hard to hide their fun ;
So, when I gaze into thine eyes, my brother,
  And hear thee say, " The field is fought and won," *
Condon, brave throttler of the innocent calf,
Good brother augur, loud and long I laugh.

He Heareth a Cheering Anecdote.

This afternoon a ray of comfort gleamed
  Upon my darkness, for there came a friend,
  Who told me that from Lanark to Land's End
The tide was flowing faster than I dreamed.
For sheltering in a shop, while rain-clouds streamed,
  He heard a mother to her child who spake,
  " Say ' Bloody Balfour,' darlint, and this cake
Shall be thine own,"—and straight the babe blasphemed.

O gallant mother! O heroic child !
  What priceless teaching in this tale is found !
Let Balfour's name be everywhere reviled,
  Till babes unborn shall learn to loathe its sound.
Thus, having scotched the gory Scottish snake,
Erin shall ultimately "take the cake."

* *Vide United Ireland,* Feb. 9th, 1889, in which Mr. Condon, M.P.,
writes : " I was conveyed to Mr. O'Brien's cell, and was almost amazed to
find him putting his clothes on. I took his hand and said, ' My dear William,
the field is fought and won.' He smiled and said, ' It is'nt lost, Tom,' adding,
' It was a stiff fight ; but, thank God, it is all over, though to fight physically
has cost me something.' "

He Waxeth Comparatively Chirpy.

My prison grows a paradise of late ;
　　This morn they took me from my dungeon bare,
　　And straight ensconced me in an easy chair,
Before a fire that roareth in the grate.
And furthermore, they actually state
　　That I no more need taste the noxious nibs,
　　At which my stainless stomach shies and jibs,
As steeds refuse to leap a five-barred gate.

My appetite returns.　Ho! seneschal,
　　Fetch me another helping of roast beef ;
Stint not thy gravy, man, but over all
　　Pour it profuse.　I am no common thief.
See how the flickering flame leaps up!　Ha! ha!
Erin Mavourneen — Here's the beef—go-bragh !

4. The Fretful Pork-O'-Brine.

HARK you, John Bully, not John Bull,—
  Since bullying's your latest line—
For each particular hair you pull
  From off the fretful Pork-O'-Brine,
For each bright thread of Billy's curl,
  That from its roots your ruffians hale,
The entrails of a Saxon Earl
  Shall glut the vengeance of the Gael.

>   *Chorus.*—On hearthstone and on heather,
>   Hand in hand together,
>   We ruthless I.R.B.'s,
>   Declare it, declare it,
>   And swear, swear, swear it,
>   Upon our bended knees.

For every solitary scratch
  On Bill O'Brien's sainted skin,
A County Councillor we'll catch,
  And card complete from heel to chin :
While if one drop of blood we scan
  Upon that pelt of shivering snow,
By Heavens! a County Alderman
  Shall in his gushing gore lie low.

>   *Chorus.*—On hearthstone and on heather, etc.

And look you, for the scattered chips
　　Of Billy's splintered golden specs,
Our submarine torpedo-ships
　　Shall leave a line of smoking wrecks.
And should your murderous mamelukes
　　One labouring limb of Billy's break,
A brace of belted British dukes
　　Shall bite the dust, and no mistake.

　　　　Chorus.—On hearthstone and on heather, etc.

But if his life, his precious life,
　　At last our struggling saint foregoes,
Maintaining such unequal strife
　　Against his multitudinous foes,—
Ay, if while wrestling for his bags
　　With brutal warders, one to four,
Our prisoned martyr fails and flags,
　　Falls, faints, expires, and is no more :—

　　　　(*Allegro con brio.*)

To right the wrong, and wrong the right,
　　About poor Bill's continuations,
With tons of deadly dynamite
　　We'll make undying demonstrations
Against your Crown and Church and State
Through centuries of holy hate ;
Until the scornful finger of Fate
Points to old England bothered and bate,

Sitting in darkness desolate,
Down in the dust, with ten hundredweight
Of cruel chains accoutred complate,
    The Niobe of Nations!
And Erin, flourishing grand and great,
And laughing fit to fall from her sate,
    At her tyrant's tribulations.

      Chorus.—On hearthstone and on heather,
            Hand in hand together,
            We ruthless I.R.B.'s
                Declare it, declare it,
                  And swear, swear, swear it,
            Upon our bended knees.

5. A "First Class" Misdemeanant.

THROUGH all my illustrious life,
 I always have travelled 1st class,
Havin' no ayconomical wife
 Or childher my comfort to crass :
But I ceaselessly flourish and fatten
 On the wage of the downtrodden mass,
By settin' blackthorn agin bâton,
 Wid my bluster, and bunkum, and brass.
So I'm *blest* if I'll thravel 3rd class,
I'm d——d if I'll thravel 3rd class.

Wid no curtain to shelter my sight
 From the glare through that glitterin' glass,
And no carpet my feet to invite
 To its patthern of flower-bestrewn grass ;
And bolstherin' my head and my back
 On bare boards, by some barefooted lass,—
Och ! supposin' the train from the track
 For one half quarter second should pass,
I'd be killed in this cruel 3rd class :
So I'm d——d if I'll thravel 3rd class.

Shall the stock of great Brian Boru,
  For refusin' this doorstep to crass,
Wid the blood in his veins boilin' blue,
  Through the windy be hoisted, alas?
Ye bla'guárds, I'll not tamely be stored
  Like a barrel of Guinness or Bass,
But come kickin' and brayin' on board
  On the crane, like an angry jackass.
By the Crass and the Mass I'll not thravel 3rd class:
No, I'm d——d if I'll thravel 3rd class.

The New Evangel.

Long weary of the irksome need
    Of making up our minds,
Our old uncomfortable creed
    We're casting to the winds :
And this shall be in every key
    The burden of our song—
In spite of all that may befal,
    Our Chief can do no wrong.

To logic in an earlier day
    We made a faint pretence,
And managed now and then to-stray
    Into the realms of sense ;
But Sense, poor drudging slattern,
    Our Chief has packed along
With Logic off to Saturn—
    And our Chief can do no wrong.

For Hartington in former years
    We nursed a predilection,
Joseph and James were ancient flames,
    John claimed our warm affection ;
But John may go to Jericho,
    And Joseph to Hong Kong,
Until they own our Chief alone
    Is never in the wrong.

Poor Erin we considered *then*
   A spoilt and wayward child,
And thought the rule of Englishmen
   Exceptionally mild ;
Now 'twixt the knout that Russians use
   And fierce Britannia's prong,
Our Chief declares there's naught to choose,
   And our Chief is never wrong.

Of old, in speaking of Parnell,
   Our mouths were far from mealy,
With zeal infuriate we fell
   On Dillon and on Healy ;
But now we stroke the very backs
   That felt our furious thong,
For our Chief has buried his battle-axe,
   And our Chief is never wrong.

Did Erin's children "deviate"
   From the high-road of "humanity,"
We lashed ourselves into a state
   Of positive insanity.
But now our Chief "blushes" * with grief
   To find that devious throng
Imbibed their guile from Albion's Isle,
   And our Chief is never wrong.

* Mr. Gladstone wrote as follows : " The Irish are a very humane people, and the history of an occasional deviation from humanity in regard to cattle has a peculiar history, which ought to make us blush as well as them." *Standard*, October 18th, 1888.

So when he wires to Rosebery,
 " Remember Punchestown ! "
Or offers to play pantaloon
 To Dr. Tanner's clown,
With loyal lips, spite of all slips,
 In accents loud and strong,
We raise on high our battle-cry—
 " Our Chief can do no wrong ! "

Mapper Tandy and I;

OR,

THE NEW BOMBASTES FURIOSO.

I met with Napper Tandy, and he took me by the hand,
And he said, "How's poor ould Ireland, and how does she
stand?"
She's the most disthressful country that ever yet was seen,
For they're hanging men and women for the wearin' of the
green.

Napper. " When Bombastes Furioso,
  In his fresh, untrammelled youth,
From the Italian captives, oh ! so
  Opportunely pumped the truth :
What a sanguinary story
  Of the thumb-screw, rope and rack,
Ghoulish gaoler, headsman gory,
  His precocious pen sent back !
What a gory, Tory story
  His precocious pen sent back !

Napper Tandy
taketh me by the
hand, and telleth
me of the mar-
vellous freeing of
the Italian cap-
tives by the youth
William.

" It was August or September ;
    We were robed in summer suits ;
But distinctly I remember
    How we shivered in our boots,
When that tragical recital
    Made our British blood run cold,
Then boil up for swift requital
    On the Italian tyrant's hold—
Yes ! each vital craved requital
    On that murderous monster's hold.

" Then what telegraphic greetings
    Fell at Furioso's feet !
Then what indignation meetings
    Packed the park and blocked the street !
Till our myriads rushed to Naples
    In their red-coats o'er the sea,—
Rushed and wrenched those prison staples—
    Wrenched, and set the captives free ;
Onward dashing, slashing, smashing,
    Till each captive soul was free."

I.   " Napper Tandy, daring Napper,   It doubteth me
              Draw it milder for a spell ;   much of the truth
                                                    of Napper's tale.
          Furioso *was* the clapper
              To Italia's tocsin bell ;
          But it's been my firm persuasion
              Garibaldi's hand alone,

On that glorious occasion,
    Hoisted Bomba from his throne :
Such evasion and abrasion
    Of the facts I've never known !"

Napper. "Nay, my friend, no fictive fancies
        With my reason run away ;
    Verne's and Haggard's mad romances
        Have not set my mind astray ;
    Yet with Bismarck's and Grimaldi's
        Judgment I must still agree :
    ' *Gladstone's and not Garibaldi's*
        Bombs blew Bomba's captives free,—
    To a rhombus blasted Bomba's
        Throne and blew his captives free.' "

But he justifieth himself out of the mouth of Bismarck and Grimaldi.

I.   " Napper, ev'n if I conceded—
        And concede it, sir, I shan't—
    What you might as well have pleaded
        For King Milan's maiden aunt ;
    We so far have got no nearer
        To the facts,—pray, have a care !
    Be more consequent and clearer,
        Or I certainly shall swear ;
    Do be clearer and severer,
        Or most certainly I'll swear !

Napper is besought to be clearer.

" But I first must have *my* innings,
　　For you're always cutting in,
　Shutting up my best beginnings
　　With your desultory din.
Grant Bombastes' generous crazes,
　　Grant his glorious Double First,
Is this man that now amazes,
　　Quite consistent with the first ?
Is the second Furioso,
　　One poor patch upon the first ?

But a hearing is first craved for myself.

" When Bombastes Furioso,
　　Napper, when that "goose-green" sage
For the Irish captives, oh ! so
　　Lost his reason in his rage ;
What a sanguinary story
　　Oh ! what whacking paddy-whacks
He poured forth of Mick and Rory
　　Torn on Balfour's tyrant racks !
What a gory, Tory story !
　　Oh ! what whacking paddy-whacks."

It mindeth me of William's marvellous tale of the Irish captives.

Napper. " If but——"
　I.　　" Now, no ' ifs ' and ' but '-ings !
　　Do you ever read the *Times ?*
Here are twenty paper cuttings
　　On Bombastes' ' prison crimes.'
When his parallels historic
　　Proved absurdly false at last

Napper would fain interrupt concerning William's prison parallel bars.

From his own clear, categoric
  Statements in the early past,—
When they proved his recollections
  Inconsistent quite with fact,.
Did Bombastes make corrections,
  Reconsider, or retract ?
Did he make complete corrections,
  Did he candidly retract ?
No, your hero, with a shuffle,
  On old Falstaff's ' buckram ' plan,
Skilfully from out the scuffle—
  From his own creations ran."

Napper. " Now, by Miriam and Moses,   <small>Napper justi-
  By the plagues of frogs and flies,   <small>fieth William s re-
Who on earth, do you think, supposes   <small>fusal to contradict
  Demagogues apologize ?   <small>himself.</small></small></small></small>
Is it make the people's idol
  Contradict himself, bedad,—
Hold his tongue with bit and bridle ?
  Well, you really must be mad !
You might just as well a tidal
  Wave attempt to tame, bedad ! "

I. " Furioso was a Tory   <small>Concerning
  Once, with smooth, unsilvered head ; <small>William's incon-
Now his lion mane is hoary,   <small>sistency.</small></small></small>
  But the rest of him is Red.

F

Furioso, for that æon,
　Acted England's Pericles ;
Now he poses as her Cleon :—
　Which is preferable, please,
Cleon for another æon,
　Or one hour of Pericles ? "

Napper. "Well, and if he's changed opinions,
　　Let me ask you who has not,
But the parasitic minions
　Of the Empire of dry rot ?
Change is never detrimental
　To the rightly balanced mind ;
Change is human—rent and rental
　Shift by laws of class and kind ;
Constant sun is detrimental,
　So is constant rain and wind.

Napper discourseth subtly on the doctrine of Universal Flux.

" Intellects of meaner measure,
　　Filaments of filigree,
Take a most provoking pleasure
　In so-called consistency :
Poring with profound attention
　O'er the precepts of the primer ;
Seized with far less apprehension
　Of the nick-name ' fool ' than ' trimmer,'
Greatly erring in preferring
　' Fool ' and ' ass,' to, ' knave ' and ' trimmer.'

And showeth that consistency doth argue a narrow mind.

" Geniuses of ampler essence
    Change their colours like the flower,
Or the magic iridescence
    Of the mackerel's dying hour ;
Arching still, o'er joy and sorrow,
    Hope's refreshing rainbow ray ;
Ne'er neglecting for To-morrow
    Their first duty to To-day :
Lending where they cannot borrow,
    Borrowing where they cannot pay ! "

But that inconsistency appertaineth to great souls.

I. " Fiend ! with slimy, supersubtle
    Feelers, I perceive your wish
My poor craft to catch and scuttle,
    You fallacious cuttle-fish !
So take that, you subtle, cuttle,
    Supersubtle cuttle-fish !
Napper, I've another handy,
    And, as sure as eggs is eggs,
If you will not hook it, Tandy,—
    Take like blazes to your legs,—
I'll not leave a *locus standi*,
    Tandy, for your bandy legs."

To free myself from Napper's fallacies I am fain to offer him violence.

A Valentine from Mother Shipton.

When irreconcilable Reds
    Turn irreconcilably green,
With their hearts grown as big as their heads,
    And their heads shrunk too small to be seen :
When they pin their huge hearts to their sleeves—
    In spite of Polonius's saw—
Or at least most exact make-believes,
    To be pecked by each Irish Jackdaw :
" Old England is on her beam-ends,"
Says old Mother Shipton, my friends.

When the Island of Saints shall instruct
    Her Sister's professors once more,
And a Cook shall those scholars conduct
    The whole tour of the Emerald shore :
When Malachy's collar of gold
    Round the waist of a Sexton is worn,
And O'Brien Boru in the cold,
    Sits as bare as the hour he was born :
And Albion kneels with pale cheeks,
    Taking peeps through his black prison door,
And pants for one glimpse of his breeks,
    But won't give one glance at Gweedore :—
" Old England is on her beam-ends,"
Says old Mother Shipton, my friends.

Then St. Stephen's sky-high shall be blown,
   And the Tower take a turn in the air,
And a terrible Yankee cyclone
   Suck the *Times* out of Printing House Square :
Then old England, Church, Sceptre, and Crown,
With a cry in the dust shall go down.

The Boycotters.

WHAT makes ye sit silent ? Come fill up yer bowls,
    Wid a jorum of Jameson, arrah yer sowls !
How the stuff cuts me throttle !—Be Gob, I'd forgot
    That whisky and porter and beer was boycótt.

For the cause I would part wid me next neighbour's eyes,
    Then away wid the drink, we'll boycótt the Excise ;
And we'll soon bring the Sassenach spoilers to bay;
    Tho', for my part, I'd rather they'd boycott the tay.

When we've done wid the liquor, we'll turn mighty quiet,
    And labour as hard as we would at a riot,
Till the pounds in our pockets like joy-bells go clink ;
    Still an' all what are riches wid nothing to drink ?

I never liked work ; but av coorse, to be frank,
    If, like S——, I was let overdraw at the bank,
I'd slave at my desk, a director of fame,
    Turnin' rags into gold just by writing my name.

You may talk, if you like, of philosophers' stones,
    But my plan bangs 'em aisy, without any bones ;
Yes, that'd just suit me ; but, arrah, be quiet ;
    I'd forgot that the bank was boycótted last night.

'Deed we couldn't do less, for we're bound not to dale
    Wid a Government bank till we come to Repale :
(*Aside*) But till those good times, wirrah ! what'll we do ?
    For our notes and our bills sure the League won't renew.

When the land is our own, we can live at our aise ;
    Turf grows the best praties and makes a fine blaze ;
Mud walls are the warmest and scraws the best thatch ;
    Wid a "cow and three acres " I'll soon make a match.

Then here's to my Nora in a bowl of poteen,
    Which is home manufacture and fit for a Queen !
What's that you are whisperin', Hoolahan ? WHAT !
    My own Colleen Bawn by the League is boycótt !

Have they clipped her brown hair? Don't stand like a fool:
    Do ye say that they've carded my Nora, my jew'l ?
To Hell wid the League !—Sergeant rache us yer fist,
    And in your red army this hour I'll enlist.

Ye Primrose Dames!

Ye Primrose Dames, ye Primrose Dames,
Who boycott Howell, boycott James,
And deal exclusively with Whiteley,
Do treat poor Paddy more politely!

If you pursue the foolish fad
Of never buying from a Rad,
Why shouldn't he select as well
The customers to whom to sell ?

So, inconsistent Primrose gals,
Get where you will your fal-lal-lals,
And let Pat disappoint as often
His foes of bite and sup and coffin.

The Root of the Matter.

[The wife of E. Harrington, Esq., M.P., writing from Tralee to a correspondent respecting her husband's imprisonment, says: "Nothing could equal the indignation of the people here at Balfour's cowardly act in cutting off my husband's moustache. Numbers of Conservatives have expressed their disgust to me in regard to the mean act. But even Balfour could not remove the roots of it, so that one as good will grow again. And I am sure that a moustache never had so many kind friends sympathetically watching its growth as that one will have."—*Standard*, Feb. 1, 1889.]

SAD Erin, put off thy dejection,
   Thy languishing spirits arouse,
And give ear to the soothing reflection
   Of Harrington's heroine spouse :
" Though Balfour may strip him and shave him
   And starve him—'tis little I care ;
For he's morally bound for to lave him
   The roots of his hair."

Far viler than Nero or Otho,
   That sinister son of a gun
Sits on us like Lachesis, Clotho,
   And Atropos welded in one.
But though we be helpless and lowly,
   Though buffeted, battered, and bare,
He dare not eradicate wholly
   The roots of our hair.

Like a ghastly and ghoulish gorilla,
    Or a skeleton, skinny of shank,
He puffs at his perfumed Manilla,
    We pine on the pestilent plank.
Yet hope, in the wilderness blooming,
    Unburdens our bosoms of care,
For we know he'll stop short of exhuming
    The roots of our hair.

'Tis painful and cold and unsightly,
    This shearing of Nature's own coat,
But we bear the indignity lightly,
    We utter no querulous note.
For we know that from Bantry to Brixton
    The eyes of the brave and the fair
Are in friendliest sympathy fixt on
    The roots of our hair.

And those roots, like the Phœnix's ashes,
    Shall sprout in profusion anew,
Till our patriot beards and moustaches
    Shall cow the Coercionist crew :
Till Balfour, unable to brave us,
    Shall own, in the depths of despair,
His folly in choosing to lave us
    The roots of our hair.

ENVOY.

The early political martyr
    Was recklessly lavish of life :

But *we* are not minded to barter
  So cheaply the chances of strife.
Lost neckties we merely repine at,
  Dress coats we contentedly spare ;
But we draw an impassable line at
  The roots of our hair.

The Land and the Rint.

(In imitation of an old song called " The Sun and the Moon.")

God bless the land ; 'twas a famous invintion
    For rearing men, women, and children, and pigs,
While the rint was for ever a bone of contintion
    'Twixt landlords and tinants, and lawyers in wigs.

But we'll all enjoy peace and require no more killin'
    When, under the rule of O'Brien and Dillon,
'Tis decreed that the man is a traitor and villain
    Who pays or asks rint in the Emerald Isle.

Law and Order.

IN the Pre-Parnellian epoch
　Of my ever-green career,
To Erin's tale of blood and bale
　I turned an adder's ear;
Forebore to prate of '98,
　Could scarce abide the brogue,
And wanted wit to prove your Pitt
　A blackguard and a rogue.
Policemen and Chief Justices
　I held in holy awe,
As acolytes of Order,
　Archangels of the Law.

In those dark days the Irish vote
　Scarce reached a scurvy score;
Parnell had not put off his coat,
　Nor Balfour plunged in gore.
But when some fifty-seven or eight
　Butt's craft had well in hand,
I said to Isaac, " Indicate
　The scope of your demand."
So we gave Home Rule discussion cool,
　But of course confessed no flaw
In the Ægis of our Order,
　The Palladium of our Law.

Old Isaac gone, suave Shaw led on
  Till Parnell mutineered,
His crew controlled, and in our fold
  Obstruction's Hydra reared.
Oh, would you gauge that monster's rage,
  Or estimate aright
Its subtle strength, its awful length,
  Its superhuman spite ;
Read a thousand close *Times* columns
  Of Hibernian jeer and jaw,
And bewail our broken Order,
  Mourn our dirt-bedraggled Law.

Meanwhile outside St. Stephen's,
  Thanks to Davitt and Parnell,
In seven-leagued boots to limbo
  Leaped on "The League of Hell."
Could you expect us tamely
  To submit to such disgrace,
Or let punishment limp lamely,
  When crime posted at such pace ?
Oh, no! the Habeas Corpus
  We were driven to withdraw,
And add blood-and-iron Order
  To our milk-and-water Law.

Then our savage Saxon fetters
  Galled again the shamrock shore :
Then no land, even Poland,
  Ran so red with patriot gore.

But I found old English fustian
   Can't be patched with Blarney tweed,
And new wine abrupt combustion
   In old bottles still will breed :
For the No-Rent manifesto,
   On the breath of usquebaugh,
From the cracked stone-jug of Order
   Burst defiant of the Law.

Then I felt—even I, the former
   Pillar-stone of Church and State—
My position wax still warmer
   Through the irony of fate;
Saw the deluge looming larger
   With no vestige of an ark ;
Climbed like Curtius on my charger
   Took one plunge into the dark,
Leaped a "measurable distance,"
   Snapped my Union sword of straw,
Joined Home Rule's resistless Order,
   And defied the devil's Law.

It beards the Lyons in their den,
   It fells the towering Pyne,
It interferes with Irishmen,
   Who vivisect their kine !
It starves and shaves your sons like slaves,
   It hales your virgins tender
To gaol, ye gods ! and even quods
   The infantile newsvendor !

Could I trust my piccaninnies,
  Or resign my peerless squaw,
To the Hangman of that Order,
  To the Hell-hounds of that Law?

No! the flowing tide is on our side,
  The cup of wrath is full :
I'll back the *Irish* any day
  Against the *Papal* Bull.
Oh soon with bliss we'll hoot and hiss
  Each Bobby from the Square,
And let poor Hodge and 'Arry lodge
  In the mansions of Mayfair :
We'll turn the nose of every hose
  Controlled by Captain Shaw
On the myrmidons of Order
  And the minions of the Law.
Charge, Dillon, charge ! On, Healy, on !
  Fall, Tanner, tooth and claw,
On the mastodons of Order,
  And the mammoths of the Law !

Sir William loquitur.

" Not being a Home Ruler, I never have adopted
  The idea of ruling Ireland by Irishmen's ideals ; "
I once dropped that observation, and I'm sorry that I
      dropped it,
  For it interferes most sadly with my Nationalist appeals.

" Without a doubt, the policy of Parnell's separation ; "
  Once I ventured, most imprudently, in public to remark ;
For I found, just two months after, my political salvation
  Under Parnell's light—and leading—by a leap into the dark.

I regret too that I commented so much on the immersion
  Of Salisbury and his minions in the horrid Home Rule brew;
For we've plunged in it ourselves, by a magical conversion,
  And Heav'n knows in what condition we shall struggle from
      the stew!

The Pot-hunter.

SHALL I fawn for the favours of this Blood and Iron sham ?
Shall I "hang upon the smiles of a brazen battering-ram ? " *
Shall I kiss the cloven trotters of a lily-livered Scot ?
I should rather, I should rather, I should rather fancy not.

He has gagged me and dragged me away to Tullamore,
Torn the stitches from my breeches, flung me shivering on
    the floor :
If you ask me for what reason I've defied the ruffian Scot,
Sure I answer, 'Tis a plan, sir, to ameliorate my lot.

For when my month is over, my wrongs I will rehearse,
Until the pitying public presents me with a purse :
And when the spring of sympathy at last has ceased to flow,
At the gory Irish government I'll have another go.

Let them bâton me and flatten me, that's just my little plan ;
Bang, bustle me and hustle inside the prison van ;
For, till Balfour makes the practice inconveniently hot,
By recurring months of martyrdom I mean to make my pot.

* This phrase actually occurred in a Nationalist paper.

William's Mission.

Dear Lady Laura,
        Since you say
  You're " really fairly puzzled
Over our present Irish Play,"
  And *I*'m at last unmuzzled ;
I do most cheerfully confess,
  What with ourselves and Pat,
Our friends must find it hard to guess
  The game we now are at.
But come at once behind the scenes
  Of our new Exhibition,
And learn—the mystery simply means
  That William has a Mission.

And this is how it came about :—
  After the last election
Poor Will looked painfully put out,
  And couldn't bear correction ;
Nay on returning from the House,
  He'd sit, for hours and hours,
Smelling, as mum as any mouse,
  My artificial flowers !

Or, with his hat upon his head,
　　With sudden expedition,
Go boots and axe and all to bed,
　　Inquiring, " What's my Mission ? "

Till I broke out, " Ah, can you not
　　Shake off this melancholy,
And put away your chimney-pot,
　　And look a little jolly ?
See ! to divert you, here are both
　　Your Homer and your Hatchet "—
He only answered with an oath,
　　And didn't I just catch it !
I fell into a flood of tears,
　　Till, smitten with contrition,
He swore he hadn't sworn for years,
　　Then sighed, " I've got no Mission."

I clutched him wildly by the arm
　　With most heart-broken pleadings,
And sobbed, " You fill me with alarm
　　By all these strange proceedings.
If any sorrow sears your soul,
　　With your true wife oh share it,
Tell me the whole truth, yes, the whole,—
　　I'm brave enough to bear it."
He smiled and said, " You're in a most
　　Hysterical condition ; "
And went on buttering his toast
　　And muttering, " What's my Mission ? "

Then I let William quite alone,
    Till, as I dozed one night,
His dressing-gown around him thrown,
    And in his hand a light,
Upstairs, dear, at a fearful pace
    Into my room he ran,
Flicked his forefinger in my face,
    And eagerly began :
" For weeks I've striven, with dreadful doubt
    And desperate inquisition,
My destiny to puzzle out, —
    To-night I know my Mission."

And then a flood of eloquence
    I could not choose but follow,
Its interest was so intense,
    Poured forth from my Apollo.
My dear, I don't pretend to think,
    After the London season,
I could recall each precious link
    In that rich chain of reason :
Still, though I can't affect to say
    Mine is the full edition,
In my unstudied woman's way
    I'll tell you William's Mission.

" You'll grant," he said, " the very beast
    A more unerring guide,
—In very many ways at least—
    Than man's untutored pride.

To pigs, in absolute despair
    He must appeal to show
If fresh or unaccustomed fare
    Is poisonous or no.
I, though I tower above you all
    Like Ossa piled on Pelion,
Have learnt a lesson from the small
    But versatile chameleon ;
And in the slippery paths of State,
    Since first I learned to toddle,
Have held the hare's delusive gait
    To be the safest model.
Yes : every man, the more that he
    Copies the brute creation,
Fulfils his final destiny
    With closer consummation.

" And then, if Darwin's creed is true—
    And I for one don't doubt it—
(For how would either I or you
    Get on at all without it ?)
Could we discover what he terms
    Somewhere ' the missing link '—
Oh, yes ! it's in his book on Worms—
    We'd demonstrate, I think,
That *that* is where the soul comes in,
    Our most Divine addition ; "—
Now I daresay that you begin
    To guess at William's Mission.

I seem to see it in your face,
   Yes, it's as clear as clear,
The soul is strongest in the race
   To nature the most near :
And that is obviously the Celt,
   Though it is rather odd
That only recently he's felt
   The Celt is nearest God.
But then he says I'd not plucked out
   The whole heart of the mystery,
Which he's arrived at now, no doubt,
   By studying Irish history.
For in our heart of hearts a vein
   Of kindred blood is smitten,
A still surviving Celtic strain
   Caught on from ancient Britain ;
And drop by drop that British blood
   Within our breasts is rising,
Until, an overwhelming flood,
   A cataclysm surprising,
It whirls away the sinful sway
   Of Torified tradition :
To live to guide that glorious tide
   Is William Gladstone's mission !

Yes, since they're far, far nearer heaven,
   He must lead on the masses
To humble, purify, and leaven
   The godless Upper Classes.

Ay, warn, exhort, console, rebuke,
    Till spiritual hunger
Is just as common in the Duke
    As in the costermonger.

" Some rogues," he said, "whom I could name,
    Who envy my renown,
Pretend my head is turned by fame
    Completely upside down :
That o'er a precipice's edge
    I'm plunging with placidity,
And swallowing every former pledge
    With ostrich-like avidity—
Romancing over Ireland's wrongs,
    And even making much
Of men whom with a pair of tongs
    I once had scorned to touch."

" But why," I asked, " exaggerate
    Your facts, confuse your figures,
And in your language imitate
    The Healys and the Biggars ?
For you will surely not deny
    That that's your latest style.
Come, you admit it, don't you ? " I
    Continued with a smile.

He answered, " When yourself a child,
    Short-skirted, shod in sandals,

By sceptic broodings unbeguiled,
　And innocent of scandals,
Were your good parents ill-advised
　To give you 'Pilgrim's Progress,'
Or fairy tales, with faults disguised
　As gnome, or imp, or ogress?

"Oh! had they forced your girlish brain
　To pore upon Greek Particles,
Or accurately to retain
　Our Church of England Articles;
Had they compelled your youthful wit
　To puzzle out of Hansard
The policies of Fox and Pitt,
　D'you think it would have answered?

"Oh, no! Such treatment of the young,
　Bright images of gladness,
Such bondage of their brain and tongue
　Were mere midsummer madness.
Then, as from children, from a race
　In its ideal youth,
Should we withhold, to our disgrace,
　Pure fiction's purest truth?"

"True, Will," I said, "and you possess
　Such talent oratorical,
None could depict their dire distress
　In hues more metaphorical.

But must we in contrition for
   The centuries we have sinned
Against them, logic quite ignore,
   Cast wisdom to the wind ?
O'Connell stated, as a fact,
   When he was in a fix,
His Celtic wit through any Act
   Could drive a coach-and-six ;
But surely people over here
   To violent invective
Prefer attacks more calm, more clear,
   More lucidly connective."

" No ! no ! you quite mistake the times,
   Cold Sense has had his season,
And hot Hallucination climbs
   Into the throne of Reason ;
While premiss, argument in chief
   Conclusion categoric,
The Demos now would list as lief
   As Double-Dutch or Doric.

" I do not say I quite approve,
   But after the enmeshing
Restraints of syllogism, love,
   It's really most refreshing,
To use my industry instead
   On sentimental strictures,

And ply the loose tongue in my head
   On Irish fancy pictures.
But now to bed," he gaily cried,
   And soon was calmly dozing,
But this last mystic sentence sighed,
   His sleepy eyes unclosing :
" The poor, without a single stitch
   Of clothes to know them by,
To heaven, far faster than the rich,
   Creep through the camel's eye."

There, Lady Laura, you know all
   About the parturition
Of my dear William's what-d'you-call—
   I mean, dear William's Mission.

The De-National Anthem.

DEDICATED TO THE PARTICULARISTS OF GREAT IRELAND AND
LITTLE BRITAIN.

["Without any disparagement to our own old 'God Save the Queen.'"—
MR. GLADSTONE'S *Speech at Wrexham, September,* 1888.]

GOD save our gracious Green,
Long live our College Green,
  Gallant and free!
Scatter the Saxon crew,
Strike the Red White and Blue,
Roderick Vich Alpine Dhu,
  Cushla machree!

God save the septs and clans,
Bless all the Micks and Dans,
  Bless all the Pats!
Heaven guard the gallant Manx,
Heaven bless their herring-banks,
Strengthen their triple shanks,
  Prosper their cats!

Oh! may Heav'n's choicest smiles
Watch o'er the Channel Isles,
  And make them French!

Save gentle Patrick Ford,
Convert the Orange horde,
Confound each Tory Lord,
    Prostrate the Bench!

God save Charles Stuart—Parnell,
Shield him from shot and shell,
    Powder and ball.
Oh! may no Saxon spy
Wipe poor old " Ireland's Eye,"
God bless the Isle of Skye,—
    Ne'er may it fall!

God save the Jute, the Dane,
Long may Trelawny reign,
    Long live the Gael!
Long live the Mayor of Cork,
Raise high the price of pork,
Long may Kings Log and Stork
    Rule Innisfail.

God save our noble Green,
God save the Ghibelline,
    Down with the Guelph :
Discrown the Ocean's Queen,
Shatter the whole machine,
Bless every smithereen,—
    Chiefly Myself.

THE BLARNEY BALLADS.

BY C. L. GRAVES.

WITH ILLUSTRATIONS BY G. R. HALKETT.

FOURTH EDITION. FCP. 4to. 5s.

OPINIONS OF THE PRESS.

" The *Blarney Ballads* show that Ireland has not run dry of that delicious and extravagant humour which used to be regarded as her greatest gift. . . . Some of them are well worthy even of Goldsmith's genius. . . . True Irish humour in its happiest, richest, and most brilliant form. . . . Mr. Graves has enriched the political literature of our day."—*Spectator.*

" Mr. Graves is a dashing and skilful light horseman. The only fault that any one can find with the book is that the exposure of the Gladstonian-Parnellite party is, if anything, too good-humoured."—*Saturday Review.*

" These *Blarney Ballads* will cause laughter and amusement amongst cultivated readers. . . . Mr. Graves's mind is too academic, too gentle, and too charitable."—*Guardian.*

" In spite of a rabid and malignant Unionism, which disfigures many of the very clever skits in this volume of satirical verse, Mr. Graves happily does not succeed altogether in disguising his genuine endowment as a poet."—*Bradford Observer.*

" The Gladstone and Parnellite faction has had no more effective critic than the author of the *Blarney Ballads.* . . . There is in this volume both literary and humorous power, which will have the result of making it a classic."—*Globe.*

" The *Blarney Ballads* are an exceedingly sparkling collection of political pasquinades. So far as workmanship and literary skill are concerned they deserve the very highest praise. . . . It may be said, too, that there is no bitter flavour in any of the satires ; that they are harmless, amusing, and gossamer productions, written for a day and of no serious moment. This is scarcely so. Ridicule is a powerful weapon in politics. The old sense of humour for which Irishmen were famous has largely died out. Want and hunger, narrow anxieties, debasing cares, class hatred, and general discontent are not the materials on which the humorist can sympathetically work. Earnestness is generated, and that quality may run to excess. Here comes the harvest of the observing master of real humour. Mr. Graves has taken the harvest in hand and turned it to good account."—*Manchester Guardian.*

" Mr. Graves, in his brilliant collection of *Blarney Ballads,* shows himself keenly alive to the follies, extravagances, and weaknesses of his countrymen. . . . The volume will rank with the best efforts of satirical verse, while no living writer has equalled its unceasing flow of topical fun. Parodies, as a rule, do not belong to any high order of composition, but certain of these form sparkling and hilarious exceptions. . . . Humour is the prevailing characteristic of all save one of the thirty-four ballads, but it is allied with a sturdy manliness of feeling and shrewd common sense that will commend itself to those who are not carried away by the fallacious cry for Home Rule."—*Daily Chronicle.*

" Mr. Graves possesses a vast fund of humour, and in this volume he has applied it with keen effect to satirizing the Home Rule agitation. His verses are full of

rollicking fun, which may be enjoyed even by those who differ from his political opinions. That his verses sting will probably be admitted ; but the points he takes up are so comical that they can hardly fail to evoke laughter from any politician."
—*Scotsman.*

" This volume gives evidence that if the National League has killed Irish humour among its supporters, it has still left some behind for the use of the Unionists. Mr. Graves writes really exquisitely funny verse. He parodies old Irish songs and ballads, and parodies them well. And the ridicule in which he holds up the Home Rule party is never malicious, though his satire is occasionally severe."
—*Western Morning News.*

" Written as they are in a temper of pure fun, we cannot think that the *Blarney Ballads* will seriously hurt any susceptibility."—*The Irish Times.*

" An excellent Irish humorist. . . . The whole book is clever, and its amazing humour is emphasized by a variety of exquisitely funny illustrations by Mr. G. R. Halkett."—*Glasgow Herald.*

" Mr. Graves has succeeded in giving the public the most unmistakably funny and the most cleverly trenchant possible paraphrases of several famous ballads."
—*Dublin Daily Express.*

" Mr. Graves has a keen eye for politics, an admirable sense of humour, and his faculty of verse is excellent. He shines as a parodist, and in this volume there are specimens of the style of nearly every popular Irish verse-spinner. The book opens with an ode which reads as if fresh from the pen of Father Prout himself. . . . We advise all who wish to be amused as well as instructed in some phases of the Irish Question to get this volume."—*Dublin Evening Mail.*

" Full of cleverness and quite devoid of malice."—*Belfast Newsletter.*

" No more trenchant criticism in verse of the Parnellite party has appeared for a long time than these ballads."—*Northern Whig.*

" Exquisite satire."—*Sheffield Daily Telegraph.*

"Mr. Graves is owed a deep debt of gratitude by all Unionist politicians. He has succeeded in throwing a ray of true humour upon the dreary realities and still drearier shams of the Irish question. His *Blarney Ballads* reach a standard of humorous eloquence far higher than that attained by any political verse-writer of recent years. . . . A work full of vigorous humour and genuine satirical power."—*Liberal Unionist.*

" Ought to do good service in the Unionist cause. With unfailing humour and plenty of technical skill, Mr. C. L. Graves has put together a series of parodies and original ballads which, in the sum, equal any verse publication ever made in political interests. The ballads are unapproachable."—*Yorkshire Post.*

" As a collection of humorous, and, on the whole, not ill-natured satirical pieces, it would be difficult among recent productions of the kind to match Mr. C. L. Graves's *Blarney Ballads.*"—*Literary World.*

" Slashing satire and genuine humour."—*Somersetshire County Gazette.*

" A bright little volume which ought to have a good run."—*The Union.*

" This delightful volume."—*Aberdeen Journal.*

" A mixture of satire and fun, shrewd, hard hitting, and good-humoured banter, they are an admirable travesty of the acts and speeches of the Home Rule leaders during the past twelve months. Quite one of the cleverest books of the hour."
—*Bookseller.*